ZERO to HERO

Please return or renew this item before the latest date shown below

Renewals can be made
by internet   www.fifedirect.org.uk/libraries
in person   at any library in Fife
by phone   08451 55 00 66

Fife

Thank you for using your library

For all young footballers

Text copyright © Rob Childs 2011
Illustrations copyright © Kevin Hopgood 2011
The right of Rob Childs to be identified as the author and of Kevin Hopgood
as the illustrator of this work has been asserted by them in accordance
with the Copyright, Designs and Patents Act, 1988 (United Kingdom).

First published in Great Britain in 2011 by
Frances Lincoln Children's Books, 4 Torriano Mews,
Torriano Avenue, London NW5 2RZ
www.franceslincoln.com

A catalogue record for this book is available from the British Library.

ISBN: 978-1-84780-223-1

Set in Plantin

Printed in Croydon, Surrey, UK by CPI Bookmarque Ltd in July 2011

1 3 5 7 9 8 6 4 2

Contents

Name Game

"Get in goal, Zero."

"Yeah – and try and stop a few today."

Simon sighed, and trudged towards the gap between the two trees that his older brothers used for target practice. He was never quite sure whether they tried to blast the ball past him or straight at him.

"C'mon, Zero!" urged Nails. "Get a move on."

"Yeah – it'll be dark soon," cackled Jake, as he came up with one of his little jokey rhymes: "Dark on the park!"

Simon was not even in position when the ball flew over his head, but he didn't bother to go after it. There was no need.

"Fetch!" he cried.

Woof!

Tilly sped away, and was soon dribbling the ball back with her front paws, keeping it under close control.

"Pity that mutt can't play for us in the Cup on Sat'day," Nails said with a grin.

"Yeah," agreed Jake. "None of their lot would ever get the ball off her."

Not even *they* could do that, without a lot of bother. Tilly would only let Simon have it. The little black mongrel bopped the ball forward with her nose so that it rolled right up to his feet.

"Good girl!" Simon patted her and the dog wagged her tail.

Woof!

"C'mon, Zero, give us the ball," ordered Nails.

Simon threw it over their heads to use up a bit of time. He had a strong throw and the ball landed well behind them.

"You really are good-for-nothin', *Zero*,"

Nails complained, stressing his nickname. "Yer throwin's as bad as yer kickin'."

Simon was ready to run if Nails made any move towards him. The eldest of the Brown brothers had not earned his own reputation, *Hard as Nails*, without good reason. He was a tough-tackling centre-back for the school team and few strikers were foolish enough to tangle with him twice in the same game.

"Why did you want me to play, then, *Kevin?*" he said cheekily. Apart from their parents and the teachers, only Simon called Nails by his real name – and that was because he knew that it annoyed him.

Nails stared at him, fists clenching.

"Not my idea, you taggin' along, *Zero*," he snorted. "Blame Jake. It was him that wanted some more shootin' practice."

Simon gave a little shrug.

"Fetch it, Tilly!" cried Jake.

Instead the dog sat down, head on one side, looking at Simon.

"OK," he laughed. "Fetch!"

Tilly fetched. She shot past the other boys, pounced on the ball and circled round, giving them a wide berth.

"Give!" yelled Nails.

Tilly ignored the command and steered the ball back to Simon.

"Stupid hound!" Nails muttered.

"Yeah, just like Simple Simon," Jake grinned. "They make a right pair, them two – the nut and his mutt!"

Simon skimmed the ball towards him at a pace that made it hard to control – and Jake failed to do so. It bounced off him like a wall and looped up into the air. As it dropped, Nails caught the ball on the volley and smacked it goalwards. Simon caught it, too, grabbing the ball with both hands.

No one could quite believe what he'd just done, not even Simon himself. He usually dived out of the way of any ball struck with such force.

"How did yer do that?" gasped Nails. He even failed to call him "Zero", for once.

Simon gave his usual shrug, and threw the ball away again.

"Bet Anil wouldn't have smelt that," said Jake. "He's useless."

Anil was the school goalkeeper, but when he had missed a game earlier in the season, Mr Smith, the headteacher of Redfield Primary, found that nobody else wanted to go in goal. In the end, he asked the captain, Nails, to wear the yellow goalie top, but that only weakened the defence even more. They lost 6-1, with Nails at fault for at least three of the goals – not that anybody dared to blame him.

"That's the main reason we're near the bottom of the league," Jake moaned. "We've let in too many goals."

Simon grew in confidence after that catch and he pulled off several more good saves, as much to his own surprise as theirs. They put the ball past him many more times, but now they had to shoot more accurately to do so.

"Has Smithy ever seen you play in goal?" asked Jake, as yet another of his shots was blocked.

Simon shook his head. "Don't think so."

"Too late now," said Nails. "Anyway, Smiffy

don't like havin' little kids in the team."

"I'm not little," Simon protested. "I'm as tall as Jake."

"You know what I mean. He only picks people in the top juniors."

"C'mon, let's go home," said Jake, booting the ball towards the park gates. "It's time for tea."

"Dead right," agreed Nails. "I'm starvin'."

"I'm going to give Tilly a walk first," Simon told them.

"Reckon that daft dog's had enough exercise," Nails said with a scowl.

"Bet Simple Simon just wants to watch the birdies again!" Jake said, grinning.

Simon crossed the park, throwing a stick for Tilly until they reached the Redd, the brook that wound its way along the back of their school playing field. He often spent much of his lunchtime leaning on the fence, watching the wildlife down by the water.

Tilly paddled into the brook for a drink, before settling beside Simon on the grass.

Woof!

"Sshhh," he said, stroking the dog's neck. "Let's wait and see."

Over the next few minutes, he spotted a number of different birds that came to rest briefly in the bushes and branches of the small trees on the opposite bank. There were sparrows and blackbirds, a greenfinch, a big rook and

even a couple of collared doves.

Simon was also rewarded by the rare sight of a kingfisher – a flash of vivid blue as it skimmed low across the surface of the water, then dipped down to take a drink on the wing, before disappearing from view.

"Beautiful," he murmured in wonder.

When Simon eventually reached home, he didn't bother to say anything about what he'd seen. He knew that no one would be interested.

"You're late, and your tea's gone cold," said Mum crossly.

"Looks like it's early to bed for you tonight, Zero," said Nails, smirking, when Mum had left the room.

Jake grinned at Simon. "No telly and an empty belly!"

Goal Role

The weekly soccer practice on Wednesday was cancelled. Mr Smith was ill and no one else on the staff was willing to take the footballers out into the rain after school – not even Mrs Gregson, known as Greg by the pupils, who coached the girls' netball team.

She held a lunchtime meeting in her classroom instead, and found that several players in the squad were also absent.

"They must've gone down with this bug that's goin' round, Miss," Nails said.

The team captain was not feeling too well himself, but he was not prepared to admit it to anybody. Normally, he would not have minded a few days off school in bed, but there was no way that he was going to risk missing the big match on Saturday.

"Perhaps we ought to call the game off," said Mrs Gregson.

Nails was shocked at such an idea. "We can't do that, Miss," he whined.

"Why not, Kevin?"

"Well . . . it's the semi-final, Miss. It's not just any old game."

"I know that, Kevin, so all the more reason to postpone it until Mr Smith returns and the team is at full strength again."

"But . . . it's the Cup, Miss," he repeated.

The teacher sighed. The last thing she planned to do on Saturday morning was to stand on a muddy touchline, watching a game of football.

"Right, then, Mr Smith has already chosen the team," she said, checking the piece of paper in her hand, "and I'm pleased to see that there are two girls in it. It used to be all boys, of course, at one time."

"Happy days. . ." Nails murmured under his breath.

The teacher beamed at Katie and Emma, who were also regulars in the school netball team.

"Glad you are both still well," she said, "but three of the lads seem to be missing – including the goalkeeper, Anil. What shall we do about that?"

"Pick more girls, Miss?" suggested Katie.

"That'd make us a better team," Emma said, grinning at Nails, who she knew would prefer to have no girls at all playing for the *Reds*.

Nails didn't rise to the bait and ignored them.

"Well I ain't goin' in goal again," he stated flatly.

"Please don't say 'ain't', Kevin. You know I don't like it," said his teacher.

Jake spoke up. "Well, there *is* somebody else who could play in goal, Miss."

"I'm sure there must be," said Mrs Gregson. "And who's that?"

"Our kid brother, Simon."

Nails pulled a face at Jake, but it was too late.

"I mean, he's not *that* bad," Jake admitted. "Y'know, if we're really desperate, like. . ."

So it was that Simon's name was added to the squad for the semi-final. He thought his brothers were teasing him when they broke the news.

"Thanks to me," said Jake, thinking that Simon would be pleased.

He was wrong.

"You're only there just in case," Nails told him. "Anil will be back in time, don't worry. I'll see to that."

He was right. Anil turned up on the Friday, but Simon still kept his place among the substitutes.

"Sure glad to see you today, Anil," Simon said with relief, when they met in the playground at morning break.

Anil looked blank for a moment, then realised who Simon was.

"Oh, yeah – right," he said. "Well, I might not have been here, if somebody hadn't come round to my house yesterday."

"Who was that?"

"Nails. Threatened what he'd do to me, if I didn't show up," he said ruefully. "You know what he's like, man. He's not somebody to argue with."

"I do," Simon grinned.

"Yeah, well – you might get away with it, but not me. So here I am."

"Are you fit enough to play?"

"Sort of – but make sure you've got your boots and gloves with you tomorrow," Anil told him. "Y'know, just in case. . ."

★★★

"I shall be a proud father if all my three sons are on the pitch at the same time," Dad said, as they arrived at school next morning.

"Huh! We really will be in trouble if our kid has to come on," grunted Nails.

Simon didn't respond to the taunt. He was so nervous, he had not been able to eat any breakfast. He put his hand down onto Tilly's head and ruffled the fur behind her ears, as much for his own comfort as the dog's.

"Wish you could come to watch a few more

of our games, Dad," said Jake. "We don't seem to lose when you're there."

"You know how busy I am in the shop, son. 'Fraid I've got to get back, too, straight after the match."

Dad called all of them *son*. Jake joked that it saved him the bother of having to remember their names.

Simon gave Dad Tilly's lead as the brothers headed towards the school building.

"Please don't let her loose, Dad," he said. "She'll race onto the pitch after the ball."

He laughed. "Don't worry, son. You can have her back once the match kicks off – unless you're playing, of course."

"No chance!" scoffed Nails.

"If you get bored with the game, Si," said Jake, "you can always go and watch the birdies and let Tilly have a paddle in the brook."

They reached the boys' changing-room to find Anil being sick in the toilet.

"Oh, that's great," muttered Nails, when the goalkeeper came out. "Does Greg know you've been pukin' up?"

Anil shook his head. "Just pre-match nerves, man. I'll be OK."

"You'd better be," Nails told him.

"Good job Greg's still outside," said Jake, pulling on his red number-ten shirt.

As he spoke, Mr Smith poked his head around the door.

"I couldn't stay at home, wondering how we were getting on," he told them. "I hope all of you are fit and raring to go."

Jake glanced at Nails and a few faces turned towards Anil, but Mr Smith's gaze had fallen upon Simon instead.

"Well, well, and who's our new superstar?" he said, grinning.

"Smiffy's as bad as Dad with names," Nails hissed.

Jake smirked. "Just so long as he doesn't start calling us 'son' too."

"I'm Simon."

"Course you are, I know that," Mr Smith said. "Mrs Gregson has already explained the situation to me. It'll be good experience for you. I'm always looking for people keen to play in goal."

Simon was tempted to say that he wasn't really all that keen, but the headteacher was already leaving.

"Must go. I don't want to risk passing on any germs, but I'll be staying to watch the game from a safe distance," he said, smiling. "Good luck, *Reds*!"

"Huh!" muttered Nails under his breath, as he tugged the captain's black armband up onto the left sleeve of his number-five shirt. "We'll need it, too, if Zero has to go in goal!

Semi-Final

"C'mon, men!" cried Nails, as the *Reds* gathered around him on the pitch before the kick-off. "We're in it to win it!"

"Hey! *I* made that up," Jake protested. "You said *I* could say it."

Nails ignored him, but got no further with his intended pep talk.

"And *girls*," put in Emma.

"What?"

"Don't forget us girls too," Emma told him.

Nails stared at his tall, heavily-built partner in central defence, who grinned back at the captain, knowing that this would annoy him.

The team's speedy left-winger, Katie, joined forces with her best friend. "We don't want to be called *men*, thanks very much," she added.

Nails pulled a face at them. "Right, men – and *women*," he scowled, as some of the boys began to snigger. "Like I was saying, we can beat this lot, just like we did in the league. . ."

The referee's whistle cut across him and the group broke up as Nails trotted towards the centre-circle for the toss. The *Reds'* 3-1 victory over St Martin's School – the *Saints* – before Christmas had been one of their rare successes this season, a season in which they had seemed to be saving their best form for Cup games. The reminder had served to boost the players' confidence and they were hopeful of reaching the Final.

Only Jake knew that the captain was still not fully fit. They shared a room and it was difficult to hide secrets. Even Simon and their parents did not realise that Nails had been unwell during the week.

Sadly, only five minutes after the kick-off, the *Reds* were all feeling low.

A long clearance from the *Saints'* goalkeeper bounced over the heads of both Nails and Emma and a green-shirted, blonde striker raced past them into the clear. She dribbled round the advancing Anil and then steered the ball into the empty net.

"Keep your eye on the ball, Kevin!" cried Mrs Gregson from the touchline.

Nails cursed under his breath. "Huh! What does she think I'm doin'? Starin' at their number-ten?"

It was perhaps a guilty thought. The scorer had indeed caught his eye, but it was her quick feet that he'd noticed, not her blonde hair.

"C'mon, *Reds*, let's show this lot how we can play," cried Nails angrily.

It was another ten minutes, however, before the *Saints'* keeper was forced to make a save. Jake managed to shake off his marker at a corner, but his header was well held by the goalkeeper.

At the other end of the pitch, Anil was handling the ball like a bar of soap. Time and again, it slipped out of his grasp and only some desperate defending prevented a second goal.

In one of these goalmouth scrambles, Nails blocked the ball on the line and then hacked it clear of danger.

"Get a grip, will yer, Anil!" demanded the captain.

"Cool it, man," Anil snapped back. "You're no better than me in goal."

"Maybe not, but I know a kid who is," Nails sneered, glancing towards the touchline where he spotted Tilly, lying at Simon's feet between him and a tall, thin, red-haired boy he didn't recognise.

Simon would already have wandered off to the fence to do a spot of birdwatching, if Ollie had not come up to fuss the dog, swap names and explain that he would be starting at the school on Monday.

"Where did you go before?" asked Simon.

"Princeton Juniors. It's in the city. Heard of it?"

Simon shook his head.

"You will do soon, if you reach the final, 'cos the *Princes* are already in it. Won our own semi last week four-nil."

"So aren't you cup-tied? Y'know, when you can't play for two teams in the same competition."

"Nah, 'fraid I missed all the cup games for one reason or another."

"So you might be able to play for us instead?"

"Hope so," Ollie said, grinning. "But you've got to win this game first. . ."

The signs of that happening were not good.

The *Saints* remained on top for the rest of the first half, and were unlucky not to increase their lead when a shot hit the crossbar. Anil didn't even make a move for it.

When the neutral referee blew his whistle for half-time, Simon offered the dog lead to Ollie. "Can you look after Tilly for a few minutes?" he asked.

"Sure," Ollie said, taking hold of the blue plastic handle. "Where you going?"

Ollie nodded to where the *Reds* were starting to form a group around Mrs Gregson, who had come onto the pitch near the halfway line.

"I'd better go and join them. I'm supposed to be the sub goalie."

"Soz – I didn't realise," said Ollie.

Simon shrugged. "It's OK, I can hardly believe it, either."

"I'm OK, too," Ollie replied.

Simon looked at him, puzzled. "How d'yer mean?"

Ollie smiled. "Guess you'll find out soon enough," he said, stroking Tilly to reassure her.

"Go on, then. They might need you."

"Hope not. I've not even played for the school yet."

"Well, this could be your big chance to be a hero," Ollie told him.

"I'd rather be a zero."

Now it was Ollie's turn to look puzzled.

"I'll explain later," said Simon, and trotted off towards the group.

He need not have bothered. He was barely noticed, nobody spoke to him, and he contented himself with sucking on a slice of orange from a tray of refreshments.

It was strange for the players not to have the headteacher giving them instructions about what they should change in the second half. Mr Smith stayed on the touchline and left Mrs Gregson to do the talking, but she did not have much to say.

"Keep trying to do your best," she finished. "That's the main thing – win or lose."

Nails caught Jake's eye and pulled a face.

"Big help, that is," the captain muttered under his breath, and then decided to speak up.

"C'mon, *men*, we're in it to win it, remember."

Mrs Gregson raised her eyebrows. "It's how you play that's more important, Kevin," she told him, "not the final result."

Nails sighed, and gave a shrug.

Simon wandered back towards Ollie, who was walking Tilly by the hedge.

"Just in case she wants to water the flowers," he grinned.

"Yeah, thanks," said Simon, taking the lead.

"Not needed yet, then?"

"Nah. Not sure they even knew I was there. Waste of time."

"What's the master plan for victory?" asked Ollie.

"There isn't one. Hope for the best, I think she said. I wasn't really listening."

"Our teacher at Princeton was a great one for tactics. Reckon he must've stayed up all night thinking up new stuff," Ollie said with a sigh. "Waste of time, mostly. We just went out and scored more goals than the other lot."

They chuckled together.

One piece of advice from Mrs Gregson that Simon had missed was telling Katie to move about more, so as not to find herself stuck on the touchline.

"Try and lose your marker," the teacher told her. "Just like you do in netball."

Katie was certainly enjoying more space in the early part of the second half. She kept popping up in different positions and on one occasion linked up well with Jake, swapping passes before Jake put a shot wide of the target.

Five minutes later, the ball was in the *Saints'* net. Katie glided past a couple of weak challenges, fooling the defenders with changes of pace, glanced up to spot that the keeper was off his goal-line, then coolly lobbed the ball over his head.

The pony-tailed winger showed that she was a good gymnast, too. Before anyone could mob her, Katie ran towards the corner flag and performed her well-practised, goal-celebration routine. A cartwheel was followed by a high somersault with a perfect landing in her silver boots, both arms in the air to soak up the crowd's applause.

"The equaliser!" she screamed.

"What a show-off!" muttered Nails, standing on the halfway line, hands on hips. He preferred to save his energy for the football, instead of running upfield to congratulate the scorer. He still wasn't feeling all that well.

"C'mon, men!" he cried, clapping his hands to get everyone's attention as the *Reds* returned for the re-start. "Long way to go yet. Let's have another goal."

Sick and Tired

"Reckon you've got this game won," said Ollie, as the *Reds* pinned the opposition back in their own half. "You've got 'em on the run."

"It's *we*, remember, not *you*," Simon corrected him, grinning. "You're one of *us* now. Well – at least from Monday, you will be."

"Yeah, right," he laughed, and shouted across the pitch, "C'mon, *Reds*, *we* can do it!"

Emma looked across to the touchline. "Who's the beanpole next to your kid?"

Nails shrugged. "Dunno."

"You OK?" she asked. "You've gone dead white."

"Never felt better," he lied.

The next thing Emma knew, the captain

was down on his haunches, being sick in the centre-circle.

"Do you want to go off?" she said.

Nails stood up, wiped his mouth and glared at her.

"What do you think, stupid?" he retorted. "Watch the ball, not me."

With the ball at the other end of the pitch, few people had seen the incident, but one of those was the headteacher.

"Are you all right, Kevin?" called out Mr Smith.

"Oh, God!" Nails groaned. "Not him as well." He pretended that he hadn't heard the question and kept his eyes fixed on what was happening in the opposition penalty area. The *Reds'* move had broken down as Katie lost the ball, and the *Saints* immediately broke away to launch their own swift counter-attack. Nails and Emma soon found themselves outnumbered.

"Get back!" screamed Nails at the other defenders, who had been caught too far upfield. "Stop 'em!"

It was too late. The green shirts swarmed forwards, switching the ball between them and drawing Emma out of position. Nails simply did not have the pace or the energy to fill the gaps and even his attempted trip failed to work. The exposed Anil was given no chance to prevent the goal and seemed to make little effort to do so.

"Looks like I came to the wrong place," Ollie muttered. "You've gone and thrown it away."

"Oi! It's back to *you* again, is it?" said Simon. "What's happened to *we*, all of a sudden?"

Ollie shrugged. "Soz, I was just starting to look forward to the final against my old school."

"Don't give up yet," Simon told him. "You don't know my brothers."

Fortunately, it did not take long for the *Reds* to score again – and there was quite a lot of fortune about their second equaliser. Good luck for them, but bad luck for the poor *Saints'* defender, who stuck out a leg to clear Katie's cross but deflected the ball past his own goalkeeper into the net instead.

With time running out, the visitors seemed

to have done enough to earn a 2-2 draw and a replay at home. They probably thought that they deserved it, too, but Nails had other ideas. When Jake won a corner-kick and was preparing to take it quickly by playing the ball short to Katie, Nails shouted to them to wait as he jogged upfield.

"Stay back, Kevin," cried Mr Smith. "We can't give away another goal."

Mrs Gregson did not quite know what advice to give. In truth, she was not that bothered about which side won, so long as it wasn't a draw. She didn't really fancy having to organise another game, if the headteacher were still off school the following week.

The looming presence of Nails in the *Saints'* penalty box caused some alarm and argument among their defenders, especially as no one was keen to mark the big, sick-stained captain too closely.

"On me 'ead!" Nails shouted to his brother, finding himself in unexpected space.

Jake did his best to oblige, but the keeper was brave enough to come out and try to catch the ball. He also had one eye on Nails, though, perhaps expecting to get clattered in mid-air, and he failed to hold on. The dropped ball caused total panic. There were so many bodies trying to kick and block it at the same time, that the ball ricocheted about the goalmouth as if in a crazy game of table football.

Twice the ball was hacked off the line, once it rebounded from the post but, when it suddenly appeared in front of Nails, he lashed the loose ball home with such force that it ripped the netting from two of the hooks that fixed it onto the crossbar.

"The winner!" he screamed, and collapsed on the ground.

The captain was eventually hauled to his feet, but he was clearly in no fit state to carry on. He was helped from the pitch by the headteacher while Mrs Gregson replaced him with her only remaining substitute.

"You'll have to play on the wing," she told Simon. "I can't swap goalies at this late stage."

He unzipped his tracksuit to reveal a green top.

"I haven't got a red shirt," he confessed.

"Put your brother's on."

Nails was too weary to complain and tossed his sweaty, smelly shirt to Simon. It made him feel sick as he pulled it over his head.

"Just stay out the way, kid," Nails warned him. "Don't mess it up."

Simon assumed that Nails meant the match rather than the shirt, but the ball did not even come near him in the couple of minutes that were left. He wandered along the touchline, still in his long tracksuit bottoms that he had not had time to take off, and his best moment was when he took the chance to fuss Tilly while the *Saints* strove desperately for a late equalizer.

"I don't think she understands what you're doing there," Ollie grinned, tickling Tilly behind the ears to comfort the dog.

"That makes two of us," Simon muttered.

The *Saints* wasted their last chance when a close-range shot was hit straight at Anil, who managed to cling on to the ball. Then the referee blew the final whistle.

"Wicked!" whooped Ollie. "A 3-2 win!"

Simon immediately tugged off his shirt and offered it first to Tilly, who took one sniff and wrinkled her nose in disgust. He dropped it on the ground next to Nails.

"You're a real star, Zero! Don't reckon we could've done it without you."

Simon was used to the sarcasm and ignored it.

"Meet Captain Kevin, my big brother," he said to his new friend. "This is Ollie, who's starting at our school next week, so he can play for us in the Final now."

Nails was still propped up on his elbows and he looked Ollie up and down – which was a long way for his eyes to travel.

"Can he really?" he drawled. "He looks like more like a matchstick to me, with that red hair. I hate red hair. Clashes with our kit."

Ollie did not know how to reply, so Simon spoke instead.

"Right, join the club, Ollie. He hates everything, so you'll fit in just fine."

Dad came up at that point, to tell them he had to return to the shop in time for the lunchtime rush.

"Great goal, Kev," he said, using his real name for once. "I'll go and watch the Final, of course, and I'll try to get your mother to come too, eh?"

"You brought us good luck again, Dad," Jake said, and grinned. "And you *nearly* saw all of us on the pitch at the same time."

"That can wait for the Final now," Dad said, and turned to Simon. "Well, at least I was here when you made your school team debut, son."

Simon nodded. Somehow it didn't really feel like a proper debut when he hadn't even had a kick of the ball.

Nails had the last word. "Yeah, blink and you missed it," he muttered.

Sticks and Stones

"This is Oliver," said Mrs Gregson, introducing the lanky, red-haired boy to her class on Monday morning. "Say hello, everyone."

There were only a few mumbles in response, and Ollie felt his face on fire as the children stared at him.

"Right, Oliver," the teacher went on quickly. "Come this way."

Mrs Gregson led the new boy through the maze of tables to where she wanted him to sit. She knew there would be a spare place next to Sadiq in the far corner, even in her overcrowded classroom. Ollie did not quite make it. A leg shot out to trip him up and he toppled over like a chopped-down tree.

"Tim-ber!" cried one of the boys nearby.

A ripple of giggles soon turned into a wave of laughter as Ollie slowly picked himself up off the floor and rubbed his sore knee.

"Be quiet!" said Mrs Gregson crossly, not knowing who was to blame. "Take Oliver into the book corner, please, Sadiq, and help him find something to read."

Ollie limped across the room, watching out for any more stray legs.

"C'mon, hurry up!" Sadiq hissed, as Ollie peered at the racks of shelves. "Don't take all day."

"There's such a lot of books," said Ollie. "I love reading, don't you?"

"No – it's boring."

Ollie stood up straight in surprise, towering over Sadiq, who was leaning against the wall.

"You can't really mean that."

"I always mean what I say," Sadiq replied, "and say what I mean."

While Ollie tried to work out the difference, Sadiq went on talking.

"That's why the other kids don't much like me. I speak my mind and tell the truth."

"What's wrong with that?"

"Because most of them don't. They often lie to try and get me into trouble."

"Well, I won't do that," Ollie promised.

"Huh!" Sadiq grunted in response. "We'll see."

Ollie pulled a soccer book off the top shelf. "This looks good. I like sports stories."

Sadiq stared up at him. "Why are you so tall?"

Ollie looked down at him and grinned. "Why are you so small?"

Sadiq actually returned the grin. "C'mon, *Matchstick Man*," he said, with a playful push. "Let's get back to our table, before Greg gives me another job to do."

★★★

Sadiq's next job was to show Ollie how the dinner system worked.

"What do you think of the food, then, *Matchstick Man*?" he asked.

"OK," Ollie replied. "What there is of it, anyway."

"You mean, you want more of this muck?"

Ollie nodded. "Yeah, we often had seconds at my old school."

"It's a wonder you're not fat."

"I run it all off," he grinned. "Y'know, playing football and stuff."

"You any good?" Sadiq asked.

"OK, I guess."

"You keep saying that."

"What?"

"OK."

"Well, they are my initials," Ollie told him. "My name's Oliver Kenning. Some kids even used to call me *OK*."

"Might do that myself," Sadiq chuckled.

"Well, guess it's better than *Matchstick Man*," Ollie said with a shrug. "Have you got a nickname?" Sadiq ignored the question as Simon joined them at their table.

"Hiya, Ollie. How's your first morning gone?"

"Slowly," he said, his mouth full of food.

Sadiq watched in disgust as Simon tipped tomato ketchup onto his chips. He pushed his own plate to one side.

"Aren't you Nails' kid brother?" he asked, and Simon nodded. "He's away today. What's up with him?"

"Sick," said Simon. "He was in bed most of the weekend."

"It's a lot quieter without him messing about in class and talking all the time."

"Yeah, bet it is. Think yourself lucky you don't have to put up with all that at home like me."

"Poor you!"

"Just as well he played on Saturday," said Ollie. "You wouldn't have won without him."

"*We!*" Simon reminded him, and they chuckled.

"Yeah, right – *we*," Ollie agreed. "When's the footie practice this week? Can't wait to join in."

"Wednesday, after school – so long as there isn't a game."

"Will you be there?"

Simon hadn't even thought about that. He'd never been to one before.

"Dunno," he mumbled, and started to tuck into his chips.

"Do you go, Sadiq?" asked Ollie.

"Nah, not really bothered," he said with a shrug. "Never been invited, anyway."

"Well, why don't we all go?" Ollie suggested. "C'mon, it'd help me too."

They looked at one another.

"Might do," said Sadiq.

Simon grinned. "Yeah, why not? Anything to annoy Captain Kevin!"

At that moment, two girls came by their table. One of them pushed the other into Sadiq, making him spill his glass of water.

"Watch it!" he complained.

"Got a mate at last, have you, *Saddo*?" laughed Katie. "Bet it won't be for long."

"You look a right pair," Emma cackled. "Little *Saddo* and the giant beanpole!"

The girls went on their way giggling, and

Ollie sensed that Sadiq was hurt by their remarks.

"Don't worry," he said. "I won't call you *Saddo*."

Sadiq flashed him a grateful smile.

"Names never really bother me," Ollie told him. "Y'know, sticks and stones and all that. I got called all sorts of things at my old school."

Sadiq nodded. "Thanks," he said. "You're *OK*, you are!"

***

The three boys arranged to have a kickabout together in the park after school. Sadiq enjoyed showing off his ball-juggling skills. He normally practised alone in his garden, and could keep the ball in the air far more times than either Ollie or Simon.

"I'm better with my head than my feet," confessed Ollie, as he lost control yet again.

"And I'm better with my hands!" Simon laughed.

"OK, then," said Ollie. "Let's see how good you are in goal."

Simon pointed towards the trees. "My brothers use those two over there as a goal," he told them. "They're about the right distance apart."

"I'll hit crosses for *OK* to try and score a few headers," said Sadiq.

"He'll have to get them past me first," Simon replied, grinning.

"No trouble!" laughed Ollie.

Actually he had plenty of trouble, until Sadiq found his range and his crosses with both left and right feet became more accurate. Ollie spent more time fetching the stray ball than heading it.

"We need your Tilly here as a ball-girl," he joked. "Where is she, anyway?"

"Left her at home so she wouldn't get in the way," Simon said. "But she didn't like me going without her. I could still hear her yelping when I was up the road."

When Ollie did manage to get his head to the ball and hit the target, Simon made a number of decent saves. It must have been about their tenth effort before he was beaten as the ball flew beyond his reach.

"Over the bar," he claimed.

"Rubbish!" retorted Ollie. "Right in the top corner, that would've been."

Simon continued to save more headers than he let in but, as the two attackers developed more of an understanding, their success rate increased. Ollie began to time his runs better and meet Sadiq's crosses with more power.

"Goooaaalll!" he whooped again, as the ball zipped past Simon's dive.

Woof!

The ball-girl had arrived, her lead trailing behind her through the long grass, closely followed by a furious Jake.

"She jerked the lead right out of my hand," he cried.

Tilly nosed the ball back to Simon, who was still lying on the ground, then tried to lick his face. He knelt up and fussed her.

"Good girl!"

"She's not a good girl," Jake complained. "She nearly pulled my arm off."

"Why are you here, anyway?" asked Simon. "Come to do some talent-spotting?"

"As if!" Jake retorted. "Daft dog's been making so much noise since you went that Mum told me to take her out. Knew I'd find you here, so she's all yours now."

Ollie came over to fuss Tilly. "You can join in, if you want, Jake," he offered.

"Nah! I'm off to see my *mates*," he said, making

it clear that he didn't include any of the present trio in that company. "Smart header, though, that last one, *Timber*."

It was a nickname that several boys had been using since Ollie's fall in the classroom, and Ollie wondered whether it might even have been Jake who had tripped him. For the moment, he was prepared to give him the benefit of the doubt.

"Thanks," he said. "I've gotta put my height to some good use, eh?"

"Suppose so," Jake replied. "Surprised to see *you* here, *Saddo*."

Sadiq responded with a casual shrug.

"*Sadiq's* good," Simon told his brother. "As you'll see on Wednesday."

"At the practice?"

"Yeah, we're all coming."

Jake laughed. "Can't wait till I tell Nails," he said. "The Skip will flip!"

Colour Clash

Nails, as expected, was back at school, like Mr Smith, in time for the Wednesday soccer session. They found that the number of players had suddenly increased.

"Been hearin' a few things 'bout you, *Timber*," Nails said, by way of a greeting.

"Thought you might," said Ollie and grinned. "Good things, I hope."

"Not too bad," Nails admitted. "I'll see for myself soon."

Sadiq seemed to be trying to get out of the practice by claiming he had forgotten to bring his kit.

"You can borrow some," Ollie told him.

"You're twice my size!"

"Not off me," Ollie laughed. "I'm sure others will help out."

"Nobody will lend me anything."

"Course they will. You've only got to ask."

Sadiq was right. Everyone refused – until Nails heard about it. The captain might no longer have been the tallest boy in the school, but he still had the loudest voice and also the hardest fists. Sadiq soon had so many offers of kit plus spare boots, that he could have worn a different outfit every day of the week.

Mr Smith began the session with some warm-up exercises and encouraged the players to practise their ball skills either in pairs or small groups. Ollie and Sadiq teamed up, passing a ball between them until Sadiq could no longer resist doing some of his juggling tricks using his feet, knees, head and even his shoulders to keep the ball off the ground.

Everyone stopped to stare at him. He looked like a puppet dancing on a string in a multicoloured costume. He was wearing a green and yellow striped shirt, blue shorts, purple and white hooped socks and a pair of red boots.

"He's like a circus act!" cackled Nails. "That crazy kid must be colour blind."

When he finally did lose control of the ball, Sadiq was surprised to hear all the applause, and at first he didn't realise that they were clapping him. He looked embarrassed.

"Yeah, great, but don't go doin' that kind of fancy stuff in a match," Nails warned him. "You'll get clattered!"

In the five-a-side games that followed, using cones for goals, Ollie and Sadiq continued to impress with their contrasting skills and how well they linked up. Opponents found it hard to win the ball off Sadiq and no one could beat Ollie in the air – at least, not without fouling him first, which Nails kept doing.

Simon showed good technique, too, handling the ball cleanly, but his best and most satisfying moment came when he dived at Jake's feet and grabbed the ball, sending his brother toppling to the ground.

Mr Smith decided there and then to play all

three newcomers in the school's last league fixture of the season, away against Whitecross Juniors, a game which the *Reds* needed to win to avoid the threat of relegation. He knew it might be a risk, but it was one he considered worth taking.

'Can't do much worse than we have already in the league,' he mused. 'We've lost most of the matches.'

The headteacher gathered all the players around him at the end of the session.

"I'm going to make a few changes for Saturday," he told them, "but I want to sleep on it first. I'll put the squad up on the sports noticeboard tomorrow."

The boys and girls went their separate ways into the changing-rooms, wondering exactly who might be in or out of the team.

"Bet *Saddo* and the beanpole will be picked," Emma muttered, sorting out her things for the shower.

Katie nodded. "'Fraid so. Have to admit, they both played pretty well today."

"*Saddo* might even take your place on the

wing," Emma teased her friend.

"No way!" Katie retorted, and slapped her towel onto the bench. "He'll be in big trouble if he does. I'll kill him!"

Next door, not many of the boys were bothering to go into the showers and some had gone straight home still wearing their dirty kit. Nails pulled on his tracksuit and stuffed his school clothes into a bag.

"Poor old Smiffy will be havin' nightmares, if he's thinkin' of puttin' our kid in goal," he laughed. "What do *you* reckon he'll do, Anil?"

It was a cruel question to the goalkeeper, who knew that other people would be listening. Nails tended to dominate any room he was in – even the classroom at times, if the teacher let him get away with it.

"Anything he wants, man," Anil replied with a shrug. "Not up to me, is it?"

"Did he say anythin' to you?"

Anil shook his head. "Never does. What about you?"

"Nah, but he must be gettin' desperate to go

messin' around with the team now, right at the end of the season. . ."

Jake spoke up – perhaps the only one who could get away with interrupting Nails while he was in full flow.

"Probably wants to try out a few things before the Final, like."

"Yeah, maybe," Nails conceded reluctantly, "but it's stupid when we need the points. We don't wanna end up gettin' relegated."

"No, but winning the cup would be a consolation, like."

"Not much of one. Still, we won't be here next year, so who cares?"

Everyone knew that Nails would care very much. It would be a blow to his pride.

Nobody asked Simon, the only boy in the room who would still be at the school for the new season, whether or not *he* cared. He kept quiet, as usual, but the next morning he found himself the centre of attention. His name was on the teamsheet in goal, with Anil's among the substitutes.

"You've made it, Si – well done!" Ollie

congratulated him, slapping him playfully on the back and almost pushing his face into the noticeboard.

"So have you and Sadiq," Simon said. "If you two score enough goals, it won't matter too much if I let a couple in."

"Don't think like that," Ollie told him. "Every goalie wants to keep a clean sheet."

"I'm not all that fussed," he replied, just as his brothers came along the corridor. He was glad that Nails had not heard what he'd said.

"Said you'd be in!" cried Jake.

"Yeah, you might even get to touch the ball this time, Zero!" smirked Nails.

Jake was not best pleased, though, that he had been moved into midfield to make room for Ollie at centre-forward in the headteacher's preferred 4-3-3 formation, with Sadiq and Katie on the wings.

"That's not right," he complained. "I'm leading scorer."

"Sorry," said Ollie, as if it was his fault.

"You can still play up front," Nails told Jake.

"Y'know – push forward, like, all the time. Bet Smiffy won't even notice."

The selection of Ollie and Sadiq immediately increased their prestige, at least among the boys. Sadiq was secretly pleased to find himself invited to take part, for the first time, in the lunchtime kickabout on the playing field. They were both even called by their proper names.

"Can't wait for the big game on Saturday, can you?" enthused Ollie during the afternoon art and craft session.

"It'll come soon enough," replied Sadiq, trying to concentrate on his painting. "No rush."

He was doing a picture of a tropical bird and finding it tricky to get the colours of the feathers quite right.

"There – that'll do," he said, putting his brush into the water jar. "All done!"

Even if his life was no longer in danger from Katie, Sadiq was still a potential victim of her spite. She chose that moment to come behind his chair and lean forward to reach across the table for something. Suddenly, the jar was knocked over and the dirty water flowed over his painting and onto his trousers.

"Oops! Soz, *Saddo*!" she cried, as he jumped to his feet. "Clumsy old me, eh?

"Look what you've gone and done!" he wailed.

"You did that on purpose."

"Said I'm sorry," she retorted. "You can easily paint another budgie."

"*Budgie?*" he cried. "That was a parrot."

Katie moved off before her giggles gave her away or Mrs Gregson could come to investigate the commotion, leaving Ollie to help Sadiq clean up the mess. Sadiq's anger was not helped by hearing a parrot-like imitation from the other side of the room.

"*Pretty Polly!*" came the repeated squawk. "*Who's a pretty boy?*"

Rave Save

"C'mon, *Reds* – big effort," Nails urged his team, before the kick-off at Whitecross Junior School. "We've gotta win this. Let's get at 'em!"

The captain was not strictly correct in stating that this was a must-win game for Redfield Primary, but Nails did not like to put his trust in mathematics. It was not exactly his favourite subject. Mr Smith had assured the players that three points for a victory would make them safe from relegation, although one point for a draw might prove enough. A defeat, however, would send them down.

Nails did not need to say anything more to their new goalkeeper. He just shook a fist at his brother as if in encouragement, but Simon knew what that really meant. It was a reminder of the threat made to him the previous night as he was getting into his pyjamas. Nails had barged into Simon's tiny bedroom and made it quite clear what was expected of him the next morning. He'd thrown the blankets and pillow onto the floor and forced a half-naked Simon to his knees.

"Just look at the state of your bed, Zero." He twisted Simon's head to face it. "What do we want from you tomorrow? A clean sheet! Got it?"

Nails slammed the door behind him as he left the room, leaving his final words ringing in Simon's ears.

". . .Or else!"

A convoy of cars had transported the *Reds* into the city suburb. Simon chose to travel with Ollie's parents, along with Sadiq. Simon could see now why Ollie was so tall: both his mother and father were built like telegraph poles.

"I didn't expect Ollie to be in a relegation battle as soon as he arrived at Redfield," said his father with a chuckle. "Nor a Cup Final, too, against Princeton, of all people!"

"I've not been picked for that yet, Dad," Ollie reminded him.

"Oh, I do hope so," said his mother. "It will be lovely to see your old friends again so soon, won't it?"

Ollie exchanged glances with Simon and Sadiq. He had already told them about the bullying he'd suffered at Princeton School, if only to help Sadiq feel a bit better. He even invented excuses to stay off school, which was why he had missed the *Princes'* previous cup games.

"Um, I'm not sure they'll be all that pleased to see *me*," he muttered. "You know what some of them were like. . ."

Ollie tailed off. Although his parents were well aware of the problems for him at Princeton – which had been their main reason for moving to the village of Redfield – it was not something he wished to discuss in the car.

Ollie was glad that Simon came to his rescue by changing the subject. "Nice clean car, this, Mr Kenning," he began. "The back seat of ours has got dog hairs all over it!"

Ollie and Sadiq had been given spare red kit to wear for their debuts, although Ollie's shirt was rather too small for him. It was uncomfortably tight, and he could not even tuck it into his shorts. As Ollie waited for the referee's whistle to kick off, he gave Sadiq a signal to be ready to put their little plan into action.

When Jake tapped the ball to him, Ollie clipped it out towards the right touchline for Sadiq to collect. Unfortunately, the ball went to a white shirt instead and, four quick passes later, it was spinning in the back of the *Reds'* net. They were 1-0 down in record time, and Simon had still not touched the ball.

"Huh! There goes yer clean sheet, Zero," growled Nails, after shouting abuse at Ollie for giving the ball away. "You *can* use yer hands, y'know, in goal."

"You should've said," Simon answered back. "I will do, next time, then."

And he did. His very first touch of the ball in the school team came a couple of minutes later when he pulled off a magnificent save, hurling himself high to his right to turn the ball over the crossbar with his fingertips.

"Not bad, our kid," conceded Nails, grinning sheepishly. "I'll give yer that one."

Nails headed the corner clear, but the *Whites* continued to dominate the game and keep Simon busy. It was quite a while before the *Reds* managed a shot at goal, but when they did, Katie's tame effort skimmed well wide of the target. Neither winger had seen much of the ball, and the first time Sadiq tried to run with it, he was crowded out by defenders and lost possession.

"Pass it, Sadiq!" cried Mr Smith, pacing the touchline nearby in frustration. "Make the ball do the work."

Unlike Redfield, the home side had little to play for apart from pride in their own performance. The *Whites* were safely in mid-table, having lost as many matches as they had won, but they were keen to end the season on a victory high.

Nails and Emma, at the heart of the *Reds'* defence, had to remain fully alert to danger, and the other players were often needed to help out at the back, too, including the forwards. Ollie's extra height was an asset when defending corners, and Simon was grateful when Jake cleared the ball off the line in a goalmouth scramble.

"Thanks," he gasped. "Owe you that one."

"Right, you can take it out of your pocket money!" Jake told him, grinning.

The *Reds'* equaliser, therefore, came as a complete surprise to both teams.

They managed to gain their first corner of the match with just a few minutes to go before half-time when a shot from Ryan, playing on the right side of midfield, took a deflection for a corner. Ryan trotted forward to take the kick himself, but Sadiq was having none of that.

"Leave it to me," he told Ryan. "You get in the box."

Sadiq's well-practised accuracy with the dead-ball now paid off in fine style. He lofted the ball high into the goalmouth and it sailed over the heads of everyone – except that of his intended target.

"Watch that big kid!" screamed the keeper.

That was about all anybody did – just watch. Ollie barely even had to jump. Tensing his neck muscles, his head snapped forward like the spring of a mousetrap and the ball smacked onto his broad forehead. Its next contact made a loud *thwack* against the rippling net behind the helpless goalkeeper.

"*Tim-ber!*" cried Nails, leaping up onto Ollie's shoulders in raucous celebration and sending them both tumbling to the ground.

Ollie had most of the breath squeezed out of him as other players ran to join the party and piled on top of the heap of bodies in the penalty area. Only Katie kept her distance.

"Huh!" she muttered. "Just jammy!"

★★★

"Well done!" Mr Smith said at half-time. "A draw will probably be good enough, remember, but a game is never over till the final whistle. Don't relax."

There was little chance of the *Reds* having

the luxury of relaxing. The *Whites* pressed hard to try and regain their lead but, if they managed to find a way through the well-organised defence, they came up against a goalkeeper in top form. Simon's handling of the ball was so good that there wasn't a single fumble.

He pulled off his best save when a shot was deflected by Ryan. Simon was wrong-footed for a moment, but he recovered to grab the ball at full stretch and held on to it as two opponents closed in, ready to pounce on any rebound.

"Rave save!" cried Jake.

Simon grinned and threw the ball clear, finding Katie with some space, for once, on the left wing. The *Whites* were caught out by the long accurate throw, having committed too many players forward in their last attack. Katie wasted no time in making good progress along the touchline before cutting inside towards goal. She could well have passed the ball to Ollie, who was calling for it, but she fancied the chance to grab the glory for herself.

"Man on!" bellowed Ollie, warning her that

she was about to be tackled, but she ignored that too.

As Katie drew her left foot back to shoot, her world was suddenly turned upside-down. She sprawled across the ground in an untidy heap, with no idea where the ball had gone.

"Penalty!" shouted many of the *Reds'* players and supporters, including Mr Smith, but the referee turned a deaf ear to such claims.

"Corner-kick," he called out, as Katie gingerly picked herself up.

Sadiq took the corner and swung the ball into the area towards Ollie, but there was to be no repeat of their previous successful double act. Ollie out-jumped his marker, but the bodily contact in mid-air caused him to head the ball over the crossbar.

"Unlucky!" cried Mr Smith. "Good effort."

That proved to be their last attempt on goal, but the *Whites* had not finished yet. As the referee checked his watch they launched another attack, which was only ended by Emma's foul on their number nine as he tried to take the ball past her.

The *Reds* formed a defensive wall to protect their goal, but it only served to block Simon's view. As the shooter made contact, some of the so-called bricks in the wall ducked out of the way of the missile, and Simon did not see the ball until it was too late. He didn't even have time to move. He could only watch, like everyone else, as the ball thumped against the post and bounced back into play, for Nails to hoof it away out of danger.

That proved to be the last kick of the match, and both teams had to be content with one point apiece from a 1-1 draw.

"We'll have to wait now, until we know the other results," Mr Smith told his players. "Keep your fingers crossed."

Nails wrapped an arm around Simon as they headed towards the changing rooms. "You did OK in the end, our kid," he grinned. "So I'll let you off about that early goal."

Simon took the lack of "Zero" to mean that he was in his brother's good books for a change.

"I just hope Anil's back in goal for the final," he said. "He deserves a medal more than me."

"Rubbish!" Nails retorted. "You're our number one now!"

Simon sighed. "Oh, well – guess that's better than having a big, round *zero* on the back of my shirt. . ."

Bully Boy

"Easy! Easy!" chanted Ollie, laughing, after guiding another header past Simon. "Good job you were on better form than this yesterday."

Simon shrugged off the mockery, knowing it was just in fun. Tilly had already fetched the ball and nosed it to him, so he passed it back out to Sadiq.

"C'mon, bet you can't do it again," he challenged. "I wasn't really trying."

"Oh, yeah!" Ollie laughed. "Pull the other one."

Sadiq's next cross was perfect, planting the ball right onto Ollie's forehead as he loped towards goal.

This time Simon made more of an effort,

but his dive was in vain, as the ball deflected in off the tree.

"Goooaaalll!" whooped Ollie.

The trio, plus Tilly, had been in the park for at least an hour on Sunday afternoon, and it was just as well for Simon that no one was keeping count of how many goals he had let in. He was about to suggest that they packed up when a phone went off, playing the theme music to a TV soccer programme.

"Not mine," he said. "I've got the sound of a quacking duck!"

Ollie took his mobile out of a bag. "It's a text."

Sadiq practised his ball-juggling skills while they waited for Ollie, and Simon had a drink of water.

"Want a swig?" Simon asked, offering the bottle to Ollie, who shook his head and slumped down against a tree trunk. "Wasn't *him* again, was it?"

"'Fraid so. He's a real pain."

Ever since Redfield had reached the Cup Final,

Ollie had been plagued by abusive calls, emails and texts from Connor, the captain of Princeton Juniors.

"Any water left?" asked Sadiq, trotting towards them. Simon tossed him the bottle. "That was Connor again," he told him.

Sadiq scowled. "That kid wants locking up," he muttered. "What did he say this time?"

Ollie attempted a shrug. "Oh, the usual stuff about how the *Princes* are going to thrash us in the Final, and what he's planning to do to me."

"Has he always been like this?" Simon asked.

"Pretty much," he admitted. "Connor likes to throw his weight about and I guess I make a good punchbag. He knows I won't hit back."

"Why not?" said Sadiq.

"He's bigger than me."

"Bigger?" Simon gasped. "He must be a giant!"

"Well – *harder*, then. A real hard case."

"More like a *nutcase*, you mean," said Sadiq.

"Yeah, that as well," sighed Ollie.

"Do your parents know anything about this?"

asked Simon. "I'm sure they'd put a stop to it."

Ollie shook his head. "I'd rather deal with it myself."

"Best way is to hit him where it hurts," Sadiq said, grinning.

"I told you – he's dead hard."

"I mean, where it will *really* hurt – on the soccer pitch – by beating his lot in the final and scoring a hat-trick!"

They all chuckled.

"As if," said Ollie. "In my dreams, maybe."

"C'mon," said Simon, whistling to Tilly, who was rooting around in the undergrowth nearby. "I'm hungry. Time for *tea*."

He stressed the last word, and immediately Tilly came running up to him. "That's her favourite word," he explained.

Ollie scrambled to his feet and began collecting his gear.

"Oh, yeah, there *was* one more thing Connor put," he said, as if he had just remembered it.

"What's that?" asked Simon.

"That we've been relegated. . ."

★★★

"Rubbish!" scoffed Nails. "Who is this Connor, anyway?"

"The *Princes'* captain," Simon told him.

"So how would he know something like that?" asked Jake.

Simon shrugged. "I'm just telling you what he told Ollie, that's all."

"I suppose, if he plays for a Sunday team, he might've heard a few results from kids at other schools," Jake admitted. "But that doesn't mean it's true, does it?"

"Bet it's just a wind-up," said Nails, finishing his tea. "No worries."

They *were* worried, however, and they both went straight up to their room afterwards to ring and text their mates. Mum did not allow phones at the table.

Simon went out into the garden to refill the two metal bird-feeders with nuts and seeds. He hung them back up on the branches, out of reach of Tilly, who was far more interested in playing with a ball. Simon tried to dribble it past her, but she easily took the ball off him before dropping it back at his feet for another go. Their game was soon interrupted, however, by Jake, who booted the ball over the fence.

"What did you go and do that for?" Simon demanded.

"Felt like it," Jake smirked. "Just came to say, we reckon that stupid Connor kid is lying. Nobody else has heard anything yet."

"Expect we'll find out soon enough," Simon said, and spoke to Tilly. "Fetch ball."

Simon moved a loose section of the fence to let the dog squeeze through the gap into the neighbours' garden. They didn't seem to mind, so long as she didn't dig up any of their plants.

"You don't sound all that bothered," Jake said, pulling a face. "I mean, you're the one it'll affect most. Y'know, for next season, like."

Before Simon could respond, Tilly was back with the ball in her mouth, but she kept her distance from Jake.

"Anyway," he continued, "gotta go. Me and

Nails are off to the park. Coming?"

Simon shook his head and sat on the wooden seat, with Tilly at his side, to wait for the arrival of the coal tits, thrushes, magpies, finches and his other feathered friends which were all regular visitors to their garden. News would soon get around that there was a free feed on offer.

"Enough football for one day, eh?" he murmured, tickling Tilly behind the ears, although he wasn't quite sure that she would agree.

Friendly Fixture

"I have some important news," announced Mr Smith at the end of Monday morning assembly. Then he broke into a broad smile. "We're safe!"

Most of the pupils did not understand what the headteacher meant, until he asked the members of the soccer squad to stand up and receive a special round of applause.

"Well done," he said. "I can confirm that the point we gained from our draw at the weekend means that we are now safe from relegation."

Mr Smith told the players to wait in the hall while everyone else filed back to their classrooms, and Nails pushed his way towards Jake, who was next to Ollie.

"Knew all along we'd be OK," he grinned, slapping his brother on the back.

"So much for what that Connor was trying to make out," grunted Jake.

"Typical of Connor," said Ollie. "Soz, guys – that's what he's like, I'm afraid."

"No sweat, *Timber*," Nails told him. "All the more reason for stuffin' his lot in the Final on Sat'day. Y'know, shut him up, like."

"Yeah, then he won't bother you any more," Jake assured him. "He'll be history!"

Mr Smith had decided that the footballers would benefit from extra match practice and told them that he had arranged a midweek friendly against a school from the nearby village of South Bringworth.

"They beat us in the league, remember, so they'll give us a good game," he said, "and it will also help me to decide who will play in the Final. For example, I'm going to give Anil and Simon half the game each in goal."

The two keepers glanced at each other and Simon sensed Anil's disappointment – or resentment. He wasn't quite sure which, but it gave him an idea. "After all, it's only a friendly," he told himself.

Simon guessed that all the keen young footballers in his own class would give anything to be in his boots but, deep down, he knew that he would quite happily let anyone borrow them and take his place.

The following day, the teamsheet was pinned up on the sports noticeboard, showing Simon starting in goal, and it caused much surprise and confusion.

"Dunno what old Smiffy's playin' at," grunted Nails, jabbing a finger at the piece of paper. "Is he havin' some kind of joke, or what?"

Jake was equally baffled – and annoyed. His own name was among those who would be coming on at half-time. As the school's top goal-scorer, he had never been one of the substitutes before.

"He must've picked nearly the whole squad," he grumbled. "That's just stupid."

"Dead right. If he don't know what his best team is by now, he never will."

The trouble was, Mr Smith was not at all sure that he actually had a *best* team. Performances this season had been inconsistent, which was why Redfield had come so close to relegation. He was still amazed that they had somehow managed to reach the Cup Final.

On Wednesday, it did not take South Bringworth long to show why they had finished near the top of the league table. Their passing was quick and slick and they were slicing through the makeshift *Reds'* defence with ease, keeping Simon busy. He started well enough, handling the ball cleanly and pulling off two good saves, but then seemed to make little real effort to stop another shot from going past him into the net.

"What happened there?" Nails demanded.

Simon responded with a shrug.

"I was unsighted," he said as an excuse. "Didn't see the ball till it was too late."

There was no time for Nails to argue. The wave of attacks continued and even the captain was struggling to keep them at bay, often finding himself with more than one opponent to mark. Five minutes later, he chose the wrong one and the other was free to control the ball and then place his shot wide of Simon's half-hearted dive.

Things went from bad to worse after that, apart from a neatly-taken goal by Katie. Simon let two more goals in and the *Reds* found themselves on the wrong end of a 4-1 scoreline at half-time.

"What's up with you, Zero?" snapped Nails. "Smiffy won't think much of that."

The headteacher did not say anything to Simon. He was too busy reorganising the team, bringing on all the substitutes for the second half, as intended. Both Ollie and Sadiq were rested, too – neither had been able to make much impression on the game.

"Good luck!" Simon said, as Anil pulled on his gloves nearby.

Anil looked at him almost suspiciously. "You really mean that?"

"Sure. You've played all the Cup games, so you should be in goal for the Final too."

"Up to Smithy."

Simon grinned. "I think you'll be OK now, after my display today."

Jake came up to him as Anil trotted off towards the goal. "I know what you were up to there. I was watching you closely. You were hardly trying."

Simon made no effort to deny it.

"Don't know whether you're crazy or lazy!" Jake muttered, before he took the field. "Just don't say anything to Nails, or he'll batter you."

Jake led the *Reds'* fightback in the second half, scoring a goal himself and making another for Ryan, but sandwiched between these was a fifth strike for South Bringworth, who ran out 5-3 winners. Anil played well enough, though Nails still blamed him for not preventing the final goal which killed off any hopes they might have had of gaining a draw.

Nails grumbled all the way home.

"Anil was too slow comin' off his line," he told Jake, as Simon trailed along behind them. "Reckon he's scared of gettin' hurt if he dives at some kid's feet."

"Well, they say that all goalies are crazy –

if they're any good," Jake replied, turning to catch Simon's eye. "So Anil can't be much cop."

"Guess we'll just have to put up with him in the Final," Nails sighed. "Smiffy won't risk Zero now, the way he played. He was rubbish!"

"I *am* still here, you know," said Simon. "I *can* hear what you're saying about me."

"Good," grunted Nails. "So you know you've gone and blown yer chances today."

"Don't care."

Nails swung round. "*Don't care?*" he repeated, fuming. "Well it's about time you did, Zero, 'cos you're lettin' us down."

"Us?"

"Yeah, *us* – yer family, yer teammates and yer school."

Nails strode off, leaving his brothers behind.

"If I were you, Si, I'd keep out of his way when we get home and let him cool down a bit," said Jake. "And let me give you one more piece of advice."

"What's that?"

"Start caring."

Up for the Cup

"The way you played the other day, Zero, think yerself lucky even to be one of the subs tomorrow."

It was almost the first time Nails had spoken to Simon since Wednesday's defeat and even their parents had noticed the difference. The house had been strangely quiet without the usual arguments and insults.

"Probably nerves before the big match," said Dad

"It's only another silly game," said Mum. "I wish I hadn't agreed to go and watch."

"It's a Cup Final. It'll mean a lot to the lads, you being there."

"I doubt it. Only Jake seemed pleased when

they heard – and now Simon's not even playing."

"He's a sub. He might well be needed at some point," he said. "Anyway, Jake thinks I bring the team luck, so we can double that together."

"I expect I shall be more of a jinx," said Mum, pulling a face. "And then they'll blame me for losing."

"Nonsense – with both of us on the touchline cheering, they're bound to win."

"You certainly won't hear me doing any cheering. In fact, if it starts raining, I shall be back in the car, reading a book."

Given a choice, Simon might well have preferred to be with her, keeping Tilly company too. At least his plan had worked, and he was relieved not to be chosen in the starting line-up – and, with luck, he might not even have to take his coat off at all.

Ollie and Sadiq were also relieved, but in their case, it was because they *had* been picked for the team. They had both been a little anxious after their disappointing performances in the midweek friendly.

Ollie would have hated to miss the match against his old school, despite the fact that he knew he would have to put up with insults from Connor and perhaps from some of the other Princeton players too. He had been receiving more messages from Connor, none of which were very complimentary.

The three boys were having an extra session in the park after school on Friday with Tilly acting as ball-girl as usual behind the goal.

"Is Connor still bothering you?" asked Simon, as Sadiq's wild shot set Tilly off on another chase after the ball.

"'Fraid so, but I'd rather not repeat some of the stuff," Ollie said, and gave Simon a grin. "You're too young!"

They all laughed.

"Anyway, never mind Connor. Let's practise penalties," suggested Sadiq.

"No point," said Simon. "Nails says it's the captain's job."

"So how many has he scored?"

"None."

"None!" repeated Sadiq in disbelief. "So how many has he missed?"

"None – least, as far as I know. I'd have heard Jake going on about it, if he had," Simon said, then grinned. "We've been so bad this season, we hardly ever get into the other team's penalty area!"

"What if the Final ends in a draw?" asked Ollie. "Does it go to a shoot-out?"

"No idea," said Simon. "Smithy's not said anything about that, has he?"

"Bet he doesn't even know himself," muttered Sadiq. "C'mon, let's have a few goes. Y'know, just in case, like."

Ollie and Sadiq spent the next ten minutes shooting at goal from where they thought a penalty spot might be. Some kicks they blasted as hard as they could, some they side-footed more carefully, trying to send Simon diving the wrong way. Most of their efforts were on target but others flew high or wide. Simon managed to save the odd one – sometimes by not even moving and finding the ball fired straight at him – but, in truth, Tilly touched the ball far more often than he did.

"Well, let's hope Anil's better than you are, Si!" laughed Ollie.

"Doubt it," grunted Sadiq. "He's pretty useless, if you ask me. Simon should still be in goal."

"I'm not bothered," Simon admitted and then slapped his thigh. "C'mon, Tilly, time for a drink."

Tilly recognised the same words and lapping noises that Simon made with his tongue when he refilled her water bowl at home. She shot off towards the brook, yelping with delight.

"Gotta go, guys," said Simon. "See you tomorrow."

***

"Up for the Cup!"

Jake's rallying cry was taken up by all the players in the school minibus as Mr Smith drove them to the neutral venue which was being used for the Cup Final. Mrs Gregson was there, too, helping supervise them all – especially the girls in the squad.

"Up for the Cup!" they chanted. "Up for the Cup!"

"Right, give it a rest now, everybody," Mrs Gregson called out over the noise. "We're nearly there, so a little decorum, please. We don't want people to think you're a bunch of soccer hooligans!"

"What does dec . . . decorum mean?" asked Simon.

Ollie grinned. "I think, in this case, it means 'Belt up, you lot!'"

The minibus soon entered the parking area of the large playing fields and pulled up near a grassy area to disgorge its eager footballers. Their parents' cars were right behind, full of family members and schoolmates, but all the same they seemed to be outnumbered by Princeton supporters.

"I used to come and play here when I was a lad," said Dad, clipping Tilly's lead onto her collar before she jumped from the back of the car.

"Really," replied Mum, unimpressed, climbing

out rather more slowly and leaving a book on the front seat, just in case. She looked up at the sky, hoping to see some rain clouds, but the weather seemed set fair, despite the strong wind.

"I haven't said anything to our Simon, but there's one thing here that I think he's going to like very much when he sees it."

"And what's that?"

"A small lake. Give him a chance to do a spot of bird-watching while he's waiting to come on."

Ollie had not even reached the changing-rooms before he heard a familiar sound – the mocking voice of Connor.

"Well, well – look who's here, guys. The stick insect!"

"Daddy Long-Legs!" chipped in one of the *Princes* behind him.

"Ignore them," said Sadiq.

"I always do," Ollie told him. "I haven't returned any of their calls."

Connor was already wearing the *Princes'* smart, all-blue strip with its large white letter P on the front of the shirt, and he made a move to try

and block their path towards the door.

"Lost yer voice, have yer, Kenning?" he sneered. "Shame – 'cos you're gonna lose the match too."

Connor suddenly found himself barged out of the way by another boy, and felt the full weight of Nails' shoulder-charge.

"What does the *P* stand for?" Nails demanded, as Connor reeled backwards. "Prats or pillocks?"

Taken by surprise, Connor was speechless, and the rest of the *Reds'* squad filed past him without any further comment.

"I'll get 'em for that," he muttered, in an effort to recover his damaged dignity in front of his mates.

"Who?" asked their keeper.

"All of 'em!" he growled.

"Yeah, but not in the penalty area again. I've lost count of the number of *pens* you've given away this season."

Connor scowled, and lashed out at a football lying on the ground. It flew towards the building and smashed against a window, shattering the glass, despite its protective covering of wire mesh. By the time a man came out to investigate, there was no one to be seen.

"How did you know that was Connor?" asked Ollie in the changing-room.

Nails grinned. "Had to be. Big kid with an ugly face."

"I didn't say that."

"No, but I was right, eh?" Nails chuckled. "Just wanted to let him know I was around – and pay him back for that relegation taunt."

"Better watch out for him now," Ollie warned. "He'll be after you."

"Good – I'm ready."

The two captains exchanged glares and the briefest of handshakes in front of the referee, before Nails won the toss and chose to defend the goal nearer to the lake.

"Got the wind behind us second half," he told Jake.

"Fair enough, so long as we don't let in too many by then."

"Rubbish! No chance of that."

"Huh!" Jake grunted. "There is, with Anil

in goal."

Anil did not fill anyone with confidence, the way he started the game, twice fumbling the ball and then dropping a cross which caused a goalmouth scramble. He redeemed himself to some extent with a diving save, turning the ball away for a corner, but the *Princes'* supporters were soon cheering their first goal.

Nails had headed the corner clear of danger, it seemed, but nobody challenged the boy who collected the ball outside the area. He had time to steady himself, look up and then curl a shot towards goal. The wind increased its power, taking Anil by surprise, and the ball flew into the top corner of the net well out of his reach.

As the *Princes'* players celebrated their success, led by the whooping Connor, Simon sighed and took the first chance he'd had to slip away from the pitch. "C'mon, Tilly," he said, taking the lead from his dad. "Let's go to the lake."

"Don't stay there too long, son. They might need you."

"Hope not," he murmured under his breath.

Simon kept Tilly on the lead, not wanting her to go into the water until he had checked how clean it might be. Nor did he want her to disturb the local birdlife. There were a number of ducks and geese on the lake and he also enjoyed the sight of a heron flapping its broad wings to get airborne and then go soaring away over the trees.

. . .rat-a-tat . . . rat-a-tat . . . rat-a-tat. . .

Simon stared up into the branches and spring foliage of the nearest trees, but it took him a few seconds to spot the source of the rapping sound. It was a green woodpecker, with its distinctive red cap catching his eye as its beak kept hammering into the bark to find food.

All of a sudden, the lead was yanked out of his hand and Simon turned to see Tilly racing towards the ball, which had been kicked off the pitch. She beat a couple of young spectators to the ball and dribbled it back to Simon.

"Good girl!" Simon said. "Stay!"

Woof!

Simon picked the ball up and hurled it towards the goal for Anil to collect and restart the game.

By the time he had fussed Tilly and looked up into the branches again, the woodpecker had disappeared from view.

"Not seen one of those for ages," he murmured, with a smile. "Hope it comes back soon."

He decided that he too had better get back, and strolled behind the line of spectators along the touchline, unable to see any of the action. He had almost reached where his parents were standing, when a loud shout went up from around the pitch.

"Penalty!"

On the Spot

"What happened?" asked Simon, squeezing between his parents to get a view of the pitch. Tilly poked her head through his legs to have a look too.

"Blues have got a pen," Dad told him. "Keeper dived at the number eight's feet and brought him down."

"I think the boys might be hurt," said Mum. "They've not got back on their feet yet."

Simon's heart sank. The last thing he wanted was for Anil to be injured.

The referee had already waved the teams' teachers to come onto the pitch and check on their players. As Mr Smith jogged towards the penalty area, Mrs Gregson came along the touchline, looking for Simon.

"Ah, there you are," she said. "Better get that tracksuit off, just in case."

Simon sighed, and handed Tilly's lead to Dad. He removed his top first to reveal the school's spare green goalkeeping jersey, which was now pale and frayed through years of use. As he started to pull down his tracksuit bottoms, he realised that he had forgotten to put on any shorts.

"Er, think I'll keep these on," he said, blushing, as he quickly tugged the bottoms back up. "Feels a bit draughty."

The headteacher decided that Anil's hand needed first aid and that he would not be able to carry on.

"Sorry, you'll have to come off, I'm afraid," he told a dejected Anil, and beckoned towards the touchline for the substitution to be made.

"Do you have any goalie gloves?" asked Mrs Gregson.

"Don't need them, Miss," Simon said. "I can catch better with bare hands."

"Good luck, son," said Dad. "I'll be rooting for you."

Both Ollie and Sadiq came to meet Simon as he ran onto the pitch.

"No pressure!" grinned Ollie.

"Watch the ball, not the man," Sadiq advised. "He might try and put you off by pretending to look the other way. Just ignore him."

Nails wrapped an arm around Simon's shoulders and led him towards the goal. It might well have seemed to spectators that the captain was giving the new keeper some encouragement, but they would have been wrong.

"Guess you can't do much about the pen," grunted Nails, and then he leant closer to hiss into his brother's ear. "But if yer go and let in any stupid goal, Zero, you're gonna end up in that lake, gettin' a real good close-up view of all them ducks – geddit?"

Simon nodded – message received and understood.

Nails trudged to the edge of the penalty area, where most of the players of both teams were now strung out like a washing line of red and blue shirts. As Simon settled on the muddy goal line, he tried to shut everything out of his mind and focus all his attention on the ball. He pretended that it was a bird, sitting on the nest, and immediately he became more calm, so as not to disturb it.

"Sshhh. . ." he whispered automatically, as if telling Tilly to be quiet.

A shrill whistle pierced the silence and the bird flew away, darting towards him, just to his left. Instinctively, he dived and plucked it out of the air, cradling it in both hands against his body to stop it escaping.

Suddenly there was an explosion of sound from the crowd and Simon found himself curled around the ball in the mud. He was lifted to his feet by his excited teammates, who were all trying to mob him at the same time. A yapping Tilly joined the scrum, too – she had broken free while Dad was taking photographs.

Woof!

"Catch of the match!" cried Jake. "Now you really are a hero."

"Break it up, *Reds* – let's get on with the game," shouted the referee. "And somebody get rid of that damn dog!"

As Simon kicked the ball away upfield, Jake grabbed hold of Tilly's lead and tugged the pitch invader back to his dad, who had come round behind the goal.

"Brilliant save, son," he enthused. "A real blinder!"

Simon tried to concentrate on the action in front of him, but that wasn't easy with the stream of comments and advice from Dad.

"Watch that little winger, son. She's quick."

Simon soon saw that for himself. When the winger ran past her marker again and curled the ball into the goalmouth, Simon leapt high to make a clean catch.

"That's the way, son. That showed 'em."

The *Reds* had not yet managed to cause the opposing goalkeeper any problems and it seemed to the spectators only a matter of time before

the *Princes* increased their lead. The next chance, however, fell to Ollie, who was more surprised than anyone to find the ball at his feet and the goal at his mercy. He panicked – and scooped the ball over the crossbar.

Ollie squatted on his haunches, hands on bowed head, wishing that the ground would open up and swallow him to cover his blushes. He could even hear some laughter from the opposition defenders – and especially Connor.

"Bet yer face is as red as yer hair!" he mocked. "What a waste of space!"

"C'mon, get up," came another voice. "It's not the end of the world."

Ollie looked up to see Katie offering him a helping hand.

"Thanks," he murmured, scrambling to his feet like a new-born, leggy calf. "Just feels like it, that's all. I should've equalised there – dead easy."

"All strikers miss – even me," she told him with a grin. "But the best ones aren't afraid of missing. We just expect to score next time instead."

It was Connor, though, who was soon to find

the net, with Ollie perhaps at fault once more. When the *Princes* won a corner, their captain barged his marker, Ollie, out of his way to head the ball beyond Simon's reach. His celebrations were so loud that he failed to hear the whistle.

"No goal," said the referee, making pushing gestures to show everyone why it had been disallowed. "Foul on the number nine."

Connor snorted his disgust and started to argue with the official, who waved him away with a warning. Ollie, meanwhile, was being hauled up again, but this time none too gently, by Nails.

"You let that kid climb all over yer," the skipper complained. "Looked like yer were givin' him a piggy-back!"

"You mark him at the next corner, then," Ollie retorted.

"Huh! Don't worry, I will. If yer want summat doin' properly, do it yerself."

A few minutes later, not long before the half-time interval, Nails took responsibility for something far more important – a penalty.

Connor was still cross about what had

happened at the other end and made a wild lunge at Sadiq, who had tried to dribble past him into the box. Connor's studs made no contact with the ball but ripped open Sadiq's left sock and his shinpad too. He inspected the damage, relieved that the skin was not broken and there was no blood.

Katie was cheeky enough to collect the stray ball, as if she were going to take the spot-kick herself, but Nails snatched it from her.

"No way!" he told her. "This is mine."

"Just make sure you score," she said, pulling a face.

"No trouble."

In truth, Nails felt nowhere near as confident as he tried to appear, and took his time placing the ball on the penalty spot, ignoring the abuse he was getting from Connor and their goalkeeper. He had scored lots of times in practices against Anil or Jake, but this felt very different. This one mattered.

Nails stood up slowly, wiped his hands down the sides of his shorts, took several steps backwards and breathed deeply to help steady his nerves.

When the whistle went, he ran forward and struck the ball powerfully with his right instep.

Whack!

To Nails' horror, he'd hit the ball too straight. The keeper parried it with his arms in front of his face, almost in self-defence, and the ball bounced away out of reach. Nails was in too much of a state of shock to react fast enough, and someone else beat him to the rebound – Katie!

She was quicker off the mark than anyone else, too, stretching out a silver boot to stab the loose ball past the keeper into the net. A defender's boot had caught her on the ankle and she was in too much pain to perform her usual gymnastics after scoring.

Instead, Katie found herself lifted clean off her feet by Nails

"You little beauty!" he cried with relief.

Final Score

The mood in the two camps at half-time could scarcely have been more different. The squads were grouped around their teachers on the pitch, the *Princes* subdued and downcast at the 1-1 scoreline, unable to believe that they were not well in the lead, while the *Reds* were noisy and upbeat.

As Mrs Gregson examined Katie's ankle, Mr Smith's main job was to try and calm his players down, but many were not really listening to what he was saying.

". . .a long way to go yet . . . concentrate . . . keep it tight at the back. . ."

Katie assured Mrs Gregson that she was fit to carry on, and managed to grab the last segment of orange on the tray before Jake could help himself to a third piece.

"Good luck, *Reds*," Mrs Gregson said. "Do your best."

"C'mon, guys," cried Nails, as the group broke up. "Let's get at 'em!"

"Keep it up," Ollie told Simon, ruffling his hair. "You're doing great."

"Yeah, you must've been fooling us on the park," grinned Sadiq. "You *can* save penalties!"

"Just lucky," Simon said modestly, and smiled. "But I hope I don't have to face any more in a shoot-out."

As Simon trotted towards the opposite goal, he saw that Dad had changed ends too, and was already in position with his camera, right behind the net. Tilly greeted him with a loud bark of recognition.

"Good girl!" Simon called out. "Keep hold of her, Dad, please. We don't want her running on the pitch again."

"Don't worry, son, I've got her. What did your teachers have to say?"

"Not much," he said with a shrug.

"Well, I hope they praised you. That's the least they should've. . ." He stopped and pointed. "Watch out!"

Simon had not even heard the whistle to restart the game. As he whirled round, the ball was skimming towards him like a flat stone over water, but he reacted quickly to the danger and managed to get his hands and body right behind the line of the shot. He hugged the ball to his chest in relief.

"You weren't even lookin', were yer?" Nails ranted at him. "They nearly caught yer nappin'."

"Saved it, didn't I?" Simon retorted, rolling the ball to Emma for her to sweep it away upfield. "That's all that matters."

"My fault, son," Dad admitted. "I was distracting him. Won't happen again."

Nails gave Simon a hard stare.

"Right, just keep your mind on the game," he warned him, before running off.

"Phew! That was close," Dad said. "Sorry, son, I'll move further away."

"Might be best, Dad."

Simon was not much more than a distant spectator himself for a while, as the *Reds* enjoyed their best spell of the match so far. The strong wind helped them to pin the *Princes* back in their own half, making Connor work hard to hold his defence together, but the goalkeeper still had to make good saves from both Sadiq and Jake.

When Simon was eventually called into action again, he was ready. He set off like a sprinter to kick the ball away before any attacker could reach it and then, just a couple of minutes later, came out to narrow the angle as their right-winger prepared to shoot, forcing the boy to steer his shot wide of the target.

There was no need for Simon to fetch the ball. Tilly was on the loose again, doing her favourite job as ball-girl.

She was fast enough to beat any of the spectators to the ball and dribbled it all the way back to Simon with her nose and front paws.

"Good girl!" he said. "Now sit."

Tilly sat, tensed, waiting for her young master to kick it away again.

"Stay!"

Amazingly, she stayed, too, allowing Dad to grab hold of the lead and Simon to pass the ball out of the area to Nails, who immediately lofted it over the halfway line to find Jake in the clear.

The *Princes* had perhaps been caught napping, not expecting the ball to reappear on the pitch so quickly. Like Tilly, Jake made the most of his temporary freedom. He burst through a weak challenge, cut into the penalty area and, as the goalkeeper advanced, slid the ball past him into the net to give the *Reds* a 2-1 lead.

It was a perfect family goal. The move had been started by Tilly from a deep position, carried on by Simon and then Nails who sent Jake away to score. No one else had even touched the ball.

"Magic!" cried Dad. "All down to the Browns!"

He leapt up and down behind Simon's goal, shouting and whooping, not caring what anybody might think of his antics. Tilly was making almost as much noise and even Mum was clapping.

The *Princes*, to their credit, fought back hard, driven on by Connor, who would never give up. Simon did well to hold on to an awkward, swerving shot, with strikers ready to pounce on any loose ball, but soon he was distracted by another sighting of the green woodpecker. The bird flew low across the pitch, perhaps alarmed by the noise, skimming over his goal and disappearing into the trees nearby. Simon watched it all the way, forgetting about the game for a few moments.

It almost cost his team dear. Simon never even saw the ball coming his way, but he certainly heard it smack against the crossbar, shaking the whole goal. Nails cleared the rebound to safety and then whirled round to swear at his brother. Simon simply gave a little apologetic shrug.

"Huh! Hero back to zero," Nails muttered, as he wandered away.

Fortunately for Simon, Nails had no further need to complain because, two minutes later, the game was won and lost.

Jake and Katie swapped passes along the left

flank before the winger saw Ollie moving into space ahead of them. With Sadiq also calling for the ball, she used him as a decoy and slipped it to Ollie instead.

"Go for goal!" she screamed.

As the ball ran into the striker's path so, too, did Connor, but Ollie was ready for him. He shaped as if to try and go past the defender, committing Connor to the tackle, then, with more skilful footwork than anyone expected, he dragged the ball back with the sole of his boot. Connor was left, embarrassed, on his backside in the mud.

Ollie still had the goalkeeper to beat. A fleeting vision came to mind of his previous miss and this time he kept the ball low, guiding it beyond the boy's dive into the bottom corner of the net.

"The winner!" cried Sadiq, who was first to reach Ollie as he stood even taller than ever with his arms raised to the heavens, soaking up the applause from around the pitch. "It's all over now."

He was right, too. The referee's final blast on the whistle signalled the *Reds'* 3-1 victory, and Connor was big enough to go up to Ollie and shake his hand.

"Take back everything I've said, Kenning," he told him. "Pity you weren't playin' for us today instead."

Ollie grinned. "No hard feelings?"

"Oh, yeah – plenty – but I won't be bothering you again with any more of them," he promised. "That's it."

Katie sidled up to Ollie and Sadiq as the players waited in front of the changing-rooms for the presentation ceremony to begin.

"Proved you can score with your feet, too, *Beanpole*," she grinned. "Said you'd do it next time, didn't I?"

"Sure did," Ollie chuckled. "Friends, then?"

"Course – now we've won," she laughed. "And with *Saddo* too – soz, I mean Sadiq."

Sadiq nodded and smiled at her. "Well, team-mates, anyway."

When Nails was handed the trophy, he held it high for all the cameras and to the acclaim of the *Reds'* supporters, including Mum. She was so carried away that she joined in the cheering for each player as they went up to receive their individual medals.

Simon nipped away to take a last look at the lake, hoping for another glimpse of the green woodpecker. He sat on the grass with Tilly beside him, and draped the medal's red ribbon over her collar and around the frilly fur of the dog's neck.

"You deserve this as much as me, Tilly," he smiled. "Thanks to you, we got that second goal."

He knew that Tilly would not understand, but she seemed quite happy trying to lick the medal as it dangled on her white bib. She looked up at him and gave what might have been a little bark of agreement.

Woof!

"I'm glad we won the cup, but think I'd still rather be a zero than a hero!" Simon laughed.

Then he stopped to listen to the repeated sound echoing from up in the trees:

. . . rat-a-tat . . . rat-a-tat . . . rat-a-tat . . .

Author's note

Many years ago, long before writing took over
from teaching – thank goodness – I used to be a
goalkeeper. Not a very good one, I admit,
but like the reluctant hero, Simon, in this
new story, I was better with my hands than my
feet, so I usually played in goal. Lots of
my soccer stories, like *Black & White*, feature
goalies as main characters. A keeper can go
from hero to zero simply by dropping the ball,
then back to hero status again after making
a great save. No wonder they often say
that all goalies are crazy! I think you have to be
if you want to wear the No.1 jersey
for your team. Best of luck!

Rob Childs

Growing up in Derby, Rob Childs wanted
to be an England footballer or cricketer,
or failing that, a sports journalist – certainly not
a teacher. Of course, he did go on to become
a teacher, during which time he gained a great
deal of experience coaching school teams in
football, athletics, cricket and cross-country.
He is now a full-time writer and draws on this
experience for his stories. He is best known
for his successful The Big Match series,
the Soccer Mad, Phantom Football
and County Cup series in Yearling and for
the popular Great! and Wicked series
for Corgi Pups.